Charles G. D. Roberts

Orion

And other Poems

Charles G. D. Roberts

Orion
And other Poems

ISBN/EAN: 9783744773065

Printed in Europe, USA, Canada, Australia, Japan

Cover: Foto ©Andreas Hilbeck / pixelio.de

More available books at **www.hansebooks.com**

ORION,

AND

OTHER POEMS.

BY

CHARLES G. D. ROBERTS.

PHILADELPHIA:
J. B. LIPPINCOTT & CO.
1880.

TO

REV. G. GOODRIDGE ROBERTS, M.A.,

MY FATHER AND DEAREST FRIEND,

THESE FIRST-FRUITS

ARE DEDICATED.

3

Ὦ φίλε Πάν, τε καὶ ἄλλοι ὅσοι τῇδε Θεοί, δοίητε μοὶ καλῷ γενέσθαι τἄνδοθεν.

CONTENTS.

7

TO THE SPIRIT OF SONG.

WHITE as fleeces blown across the hollow heaven
  Fold on fold thy garment wraps thy shining limbs;
Deep thy gaze as morning's flamed thro' vapors riven,
  Bright thine hair as day's that up the ether swims.
Surely I have seen the majesty and wonder,
  Beauty, might, and splendor of the soul of song;
Surely I have felt the spell that lifts asunder
  Soul from body, when lips faint and thought is strong;
      Surely I have heard
      The ample silence stirred
By intensest music from no throat of bird:—
      Smitten down before thy feet
      From the paths of heaven sweet,
Lowly I await the song upon my lips conferred.

9

ORION.

Two mighty arms of thunder-cloven rock
Stretched ever westward toward the setting sun,
And took into their ancient scarred embrace
A laughing valley and a crooning bay.
The gods had stilled them in their primal throes,
And broken down their writhed extremities
Sheer to the open sea.   And now pine-belts
And strayed fir-copses lined their shaggy sides ;
And inland toward the island's quiet heart
White torrents cleft the screens, and answered each
To other from the high cliffs closer drawn,
Kept ever brimming from eternal caves
In azure deeps of snow, and feeding full
A strong, swift river.   And the river flowed
With tumult, till it caught the mighty speech
Rolled upward from the ocean, when it paused,
And hushed its rapid song in reverence,
And wound slow-footed through the summer vale,
And met its sovereign with majestic calm.

The sunset with its red and purple skirts
Hung softly o'er the bay, whose rippled breast
Flushed crimson, and the froth-streaks round the beach
Were glowing pink. The sands burned ruddy gold,
And foot-marks crossing them lay sharp and black.
A flood of purple glory swept the shores,
And spread upon the vineyards, and the groves
Of olives round the river-banks, and clothed
The further matted jungles; whence it climbed
The ragged scaurs and jagg'd ravines, until
It lay a splendor on the endless snow.

Where the slow swirls were swallowed in the tide,
Some stone-throws from the stream's mouth, there the
         sward
Stretched thick and starry from the ridge's foot
Down to the waves' wet limits, scattering off
Across the red sand level stunted tufts
Of yellow beach-grass, whose brown panicles
Wore garlands of blown foam. Amidst the slope
Three sacred laurels drooped their dark-green boughs
About a high-piled altar. There the king,
Œnopion, to whose sceptre bowed with awe
The people dwellers in the steep-shored Chios,
Stood praying westward; in his outstretched hand
The griding knife, well whetted, clothed with dread.

The royal priest's dark tresses, made aware
Of coming winter by some autumn snows,
Hung down his blue-dyed mantle, which he girt
Up seemly for the sacrifice ; a beard,
Short, black, and silken, clothed his lips and chin ;
Beneath deep brows his keen eyes lurked half hid,
And never rested : now they drank the stream
Poured from the fiery sunset's sunken springs.
A supplication moved his silent lips,
Swift-winged to seek Apollo, and beseech
Regard unto the rites e'en now begun.
Anon he dropped his arm ; and straight the youths,
Chosen of Chios' fairest race, upbore
The victim to the pile,—a tawny wolf,
Blood-stained, fast bound in pliant withes, fed fat
On many a bleating spoil of careless folds,
His red tongue lolling from his fangèd jaws,
His eyes, inflamed, shrinking with terror and hate,
His writhen sinews strained convulsively.

Meanwhile from out a neighbor gorge, which spake
Rough torrent-thunders through its cloak of pines,
Along the shore came one who seemed to wear
The grandeur of the mountains for a robe,
The torrent's strength for girdle, and for crown
The sea's calm for dread fury capable,—

A Hunter laden with the spotted pride
Of kingly beasts before not dared of men,—
And stood without the laurels' sacred shade,
Which his large presence deepened. When the knife
Let blood well-pleasing to Apollo forth
The victim's gasping throat,—who yet cried not,
But glared still hate upon his murderers
And died uncraven,—then the Hunter bent
His godlike head with awe unto the gods,
And so kept bowed, the while the King drew forth
Wine from a full skin-bottle nigh and poured
A beaded, dark libation. Then he raised
His head again,—like a tall pine that bends
Unto a sudden blast, and so keeps bent
Some moments, till the tempest passes by,—
And cast his burden down before the King,
And said,—

      "With skins of lions, leopards, bears,
Lynxes, and wolves, I come, O King, fulfilling
My pledge, and seeking the delayed fulfilling
Of some long hopes. For now the mountain lairs
Are empty, and the valley folds secure.
The inland jungles shall be vexed no more
With muffled roarings through the cloudy night,
And heavy splashings in the misty pools.
The echo-peopled crags shall howl no more

With hungry yelpings 'mid the hoary firs.
The breeding ewe in the thicket will not wake
With wolves' teeth at her throat, nor drinking bull
Bellow in vain beneath the leopard's paw.
Your maidens will not fear to quit by night
Their cottages to meet their shepherd lads ;
And these shall leave safe flocks, and have no need
Of blazing fagots.   Nor without some toils
Are these things so.   For mighty beasts did yield
Their ornament up most reluctantly ;
And some did grievous battle.   But the pledge
And surety of a blissful harborage,
Whither through buffets rude I needs must fare,
Made heavy labors light.   And if, hard pressed,
My knees perchance waxed faint, or mine eyes dim,
The strong earth stayed me, and the unbowed hills,
The wide air, and the ever-joyous sun,
And free sea leaping up beneath the sun,—
All were to me for kindly ministrants,
And lent glad service to their last-born,—man,
Whom, reverent, the gods, too, favored well.
And if to me, sleepless, alone, by night
Came phantoms from polluted spots, and shades
Unfettered, wavering round my cliff-edged couch,
Fain to aghast me ; them I heeded not,
As not worth heed.   For there the deep-eyed Night

Looked down on me; unflagging voices called
From unpent waters falling; tireless wings
Of long winds bare me tongueless messages
From star-consulting, silent pinnacles;
And breadth, and depth, and stillness fathered me.
But now, O King, seeing I have at cost
Of no slight labor done thy rugged hest,
And seeing hard strife should win sweet favors, grant
The good long wrought for, that amid the groves
And sunny vineyards I may drink deep draughts
Of Love's skilled mixing, and of sweet mouth's gift
Of maiden-lipped, snow-breasted Merope."

So sped the wingéd words.   And thus the King,
Œnopion, to whose sceptre bowed with awe
The people, dwellers in the steep-shored Chios:
"Great honor hast thou won and shalt possess,
And I will pay thee to the uttermost.
Thy couch this night be softer, and more blest
Thy visions,"—but in subtlety he spake,
And went apart a little from the place,
And filled with sullen wine two cups, well wrought.
But one he tinctured with a Colchian drug
And gave his guest to drink, with honeyed words,
But crooked, serpent-smooth,—"Drink this, in pledge
Of those deep draughts for which thou art athirst.

And now I go to bid the maid be glad
And make all ready. Rest thee here with these,
And I will come and fetch thee.'' And he went
Up from the shore and in among the vines,
Until his mantle gleamed athwart the lanes
Of sunset through the far, gray olive-groves.
The Hunter turned, and heeded not the men,
But went apart close by the sleepless sea
And sat him down, because his eyes were dim,
And his head heavy, and his sinews faint.

And now it was about the set of sun,
And the west sea-line with its quivering rim
Had hid the sun-god's curls. A sanguine mist
Crept up, and to the Hunter's heavy eyes
Became as if his eyes were filled with blood.
He guessed the traitorous cup, and his great heart
Was hot, his throat was hot ; but heavier grew
His head, and he sank back upon the sand,
Nor saw the light go out across the sea,
Nor heard the eagle scream among the crags,
Nor stealthy laughter echo up the shore,
Nor the slow ripple break about his feet.

The deep-eyed Night drew down to comfort him,
And lifted her great lids and mourned for him,
Foreknowing all his woe, and herself weak

To bend for him the indomitable fates;
And heavier dews wet all the trees and fields;
And sighs cool-drawn from infinite wells of space
Breathed round him; and from forth the unbowed hills
Came strength, and from the ocean essences
And influences to commune with him,
But found his spirit blind, and dumb, and deaf,
Not eager and expectant, as of old,
At every portal of the sleepless mind.

But hark! what feet are these that stir the vines
Beneath the big, sweet-smelling grape-clusters?
What feet are these that leave the muffling grass
And crush the shingle sharply up the beach?
Out of the foamless sea a heavy fog
Steamed up, rolled in on all the island shores,
But heavier, denser, like a cloak, where lay
The Hunter; and the darkness gathered thick,
More thick the fog and darkness where he lay,—
Like as a mother folds more close her child
At night when sudden street-brawl jars her dreams.
But now the folding vapors veiled him not,
The ineffectual darkness hid him not,
For one came with the King and bare a torch,
And stood beside the Hunter where he lay;
And all the darkness shuddered and fled back

Sullenly into the grim-visaged crags,
Beneath their battered foreheads; and the fog
Crept up a chilly horror round the King,
Made huge the writhed and frowning mountain-brows,
Till cliff, and cloud, and chaos of thick night
Toppled about the place, and each small sound
Of footstep or of stealthy whisper rang
Tortured and shrill within the cavernous hollows.
Before the King, before the torch-bearer,
Stood one beside the Hunter's head,—a slave
Beside the god-begotten,—and he bare
Back with one arm his cloak, and in his hand
He bare a cup—with suchlike juice in it
As slew Alcmena's son—above the face,
The strong, white, godlike face, more deathly white
Even than death; then into each close lid
He dropped the poison with a loathing hand,
While he whose light made manifest the deed
Winced in his eyes and saw not, would not see,
Those eyes that knew not of their light gone out.
And heavy drops stood forth on all the rocks,
And ocean moaned unseen beneath the fog;
But the King laughed—not loud—and drew his cloak
Closer about him, and went up the beach,
And they two with him.
                              Now the fog rolled back

And a low moon came out across the sea,
And o'er the sea flocked out the pasturing stars,
And still he lay upon the trodden sand,
And still the ripple brake about his feet.
So moved the burdened hours toward the dawn ;
But suddenly their burden was forgot,
For music welled from out the throbbing waves,
And melody filled all the silver air.
And silver shoulders under wondrous gold
Of dripping tresses brake the shining waste
Whence came the maids beloved of Doris, fair
As stars and lovely for the stars to see,
And stood and mourned about the Hunter there,—
And curséd were his eyes that could not see.
And had he seen as grievous were his case,
Blinded with love and stricken with delight.
So came they weeping, and their yellow hair
Fell round them, while they smote their lyres, and
      sang :

     " O god-begotten   Strophe A.
          And dear to all the gods !
               For thee quick-dropping tears
                   Make heavy our eyes and hot.
       Be he of gods forgotten
             That smote thee, their gifts as rods
                 To scourge him all his years,
                     Sparing him not.

" For thee the long-heaving   Antistrophe A.
    Ocean, fruitful of foam,
      Groaned in his depths and was sore
        Troubled, grieving for thee.
  Grew Clotho sick of her weaving,
    And the fury of storms that come
      Out of the wilderness hoar
       Went pitying thee.

" For thee the all-bearing   Strophe B.
    Mother, the bountiful Earth,
      Who hath borne no fairer son
        In her kindly bosom and broad,
  Will not be comforted, wearing
    Thy pain like her labor of birth,
      And hath veiled her in vapors as one
       Stricken down, overawed.

" For thee the all-covering   Antistrophe B.
    Night, the comforting mother,
      Wept round thee pitifully
        Nor withheld her compassionate hands ;
  And sleep from her wings low-hovering
    Fell kindly and sweet to no other
      Between the unharvested sky
       And the harvested lands.

" We all are made heavy of heart, we weep with thee, sore with
    thy sorrow,—
The Sea to its uttermost part, the Night from the dusk to the morrow,

The unplumbed spaces of Air, the unharnessed might of the Wind,
The Sun that outshaketh his hair before his incoming, behind
His outgoing, and laughs, seeing all that is, or hath been, or shall
    be,
The unflagging Waters that fall from their well-heads soon to the
    sea,
The high Rocks barren at even, at morning clothed with the rime ;
The strong Hills propping up heaven, made fast in their place for
    all time ;
Withal the abiding Earth, the fruitful mother and kindly,
Who apportions plenty and dearth, nor withholds from the least
    thing blindly,
With suchlike pity would hide thy reverent eyes indeed
Wherewith the twin Aloides fain she would hide at their need :
But they withstood not Apollo, they brake through to Hades,
    o'erthrown ;
But thee the high gods follow with favor, kind to their own ;
For of thee they have lacked not vows, nor yellow honey, nor oil,
Nor the first fruit red on the boughs, nor white meal sifted with toil,
Nor gladdening wine, nor savor of thighs with the fat burned
    pure,—
Therefore now of their favor this ill thing shall not endure ;
It endures but a little, seeing the gods make ready their mercy,
Giving for thy well-being a skilfuller goddess than Circe,
For the putting away of thy trouble, the setting far off of thy pain,
And she shall repay thee double, making thy loss thy gain.
But come, for the night fulfils, the gray in the sky gives warning ;—
Then get thee up to the hills and thou shalt behold the MORNING."

The Hunter stirred ; and all the long gray shore
Lay empty, and the ripple whispered not,

Awed by the wide-spread silence.　Then he rose,
Groping, and strove to put aside the night
That clung beneath his eyelids,—till he knew,
And his whole heart sank, knowing.　Then his voice
Brake thus from out his utter misery
(The while a sound went,—" Get thee up to the hills ;
Thou shalt behold the morning ;" but he heard not) :
" Oh, black night, black forever ! No light forever !
Oh, long, long night, just fallen to hang forever,
Never to break nor lighten !　Whose the heart
That dared it ?　Whose the hateful thought ?　What
　　hand
Wrought me this curse, dealt me this ruin, this woe
Unutterable, pitiless, unmeasured,—
Put out my light, portioned me night forever ?
Oh ye that die not, ye that suffer not,
Gods that are mindful, seeing good and evil !
If ever unto you have risen a savor
Acceptable, of honey, and oil, and wine,
Me offering ; and if a frequent smoke
Have circled up to heaven from me to you
Acceptable, of spotless hecatombs ;
And if from vows fulfilled and reverence
Be favor in your sight,—then hear my prayer,
And soon be it accomplished : let the hand
Wither that wrought me this, the brain that planned

Rave and henceforth be mocked and plagued of devils,
Let every good be turned for him to gall,
And those his heart most cherishes become
A horror, till he flee from them as fiends.
But is this pain forever, this my night
Eternal? Thou that mad'st the day and night,
Make thou a day for me! O Earth, my mother,
All bountiful, all pitiful, take heed
Into what evil on thy breast hath fallen
Thy son! O sleepless sea, behold my woe!
O air all-folding, stars immovable,
With everlasting contemplation wise,
Know ye no remedy? Forests and fields,
Tempests untiring, streams, and steadfast hills,
Flame-riven caverns, hear me, for ye know me!
Tell me; I hearken." And his bended head
Besought the rocks.

                         "Thou shalt behold the morning,"
Brake clearly on the ample-bosomed silence,
And straight begot as many widening waves
As doth a pebble on a resting lake.
The echoes hurtled inland, startling all
The olive-groves and vineyards, rippling up
The green foot-hills, and lapping faint and low
About the low fir-copses; then they reached
The upper gorges, dying in that region,—

Region of sounding pines and cataracts
Impregnable to silence. Then, again,
Even in the lifting of his head, and making
Thanksgiving with mute lips, clear, far, and fine,
Out of the vaporous raiment round their tops
Came comfort from the hills:

                "Up to the hills;
Thou shalt behold the morning!"

                        Then he bowed
With godlike reverence, reverencing the gods
And ancient powers that watched him, and made quick
His sense to their communion.

                        Now a sound
Of hammers rose behind a jagged cape
Not many paces hence, with windy roar
Of new-awakened fire. With pain and toil,
Groping and staggering, hands, and knees, and feet
Bruised with the crags, and faint, he came where men
Wrought arms and forged the glowing bronze for war.
There one came forth to meet him; him he took
Upon his kingly shoulder, and him bade
Of courtesy to be to him for eyes,
To guide his feet that quickly he might fare
To the hill-crests, or ere the fiery flower
Of dawn bloomed fully.

                So they two went thus

Up from the sombre, bitter-breathing sea,
Beside the river, o'er the slumbrous sward
Gossamer-spread, dew-drenched, and in among
The vineyards and the olives. The fresh earth
Heavy about his feet, the bursting wealth
Of big grape-bunches, and the cool, green coils
Of dripping vines breathed richly. Swift they moved
'Mid gnarléd trunks and still, gray stretch of leaves,
Without a sound save of wet twigs snapped dully   ·
Or flit of startled bird. And now their way
They kept with toil, fallen on toilsome ways,—
Up shattered slopes half-clothed with juniper,
Through ragged-floored ravines, whose blasted scars
Held mighty pines root-fast in their black depths,
Still climbing, till a keen wind met them full
From eastward breathed, free-scented from the brine.
His laboring feet stood still, and while his lips
Drank the clear wind, his guide, descending home,
Left him alone facing the gates of dawn.

The cliffs are rent, and through the eternal chasm
A far-heard moan of many cataracts,
With nearer, ceaseless murmur of the pines,
Came with the east wind, whilst the herald gold
From cloven pinnacles on either hand
On gradual wings sank to that airy glen;

And many-echoed dash of many waves
Rose dimly from the cliff-base where they brake,
Far down, unseen; and the wide sea spread wan
In the pale dawn-tide, limitless, unportioned—
Aye sentinelled by these vast rocky brows
Defaced and stern with unforgotten fires.

But he, intent, leaned toward the gates of dawn
With suppliant face, unseeing, and the wind
Blew back from either brow his hair and cooled
His eyes that burned with that so foul dishonor
Late wrought upon them, whispering many things
Into his inmost soul.   Sudden the day
Brake full.   The healing of its radiance fell
Upon his eyes, and straight his sightless eyes
Were opened.   All the morning's majesty
And mystery of loveliness lay bare
Before him; all the limitless blue sea
Brightening with laughter many a league around,
Wind-wrinkled, keel-uncloven, far below;
And far above the bright sky-neighboring peaks;
And all around the broken precipices,
Cleft-rooted pines swung over falling foam,
And silver vapors flushed with the wide flood
Of crimson slanted from the opening east
Well ranked, the vanguard of the day,—all these

Invited him, but these he heeded not.
For there beside him, veiléd in a mist
Where—through the enfolded splendor issued forth,—
As delicate music unto one asleep
Through mist of dreams flows softly,—all her hair
A mist of gold flung down about her feet,
Her dewy, cool, pink fingers parting it
Till glowing lips, and half-seen snowy curves
Like Parian stone, unnerved him, waited SHE,—
Than Circe skilfuller to put away
His pain, to set his sorrow afar off,—
Eos, with warm heart warm for *him*.   His toils
Endured in vain, his great deeds wrought in vain,
His bitter pain, Œnopion's house accurst,
And even his sweet revenge, he recked not of;
But gave his heart up straightway unto love.

Now Delos lay a great way off, and thither
They two rejoicing went across the sea.
And under their swift feet, which the wave kissed
But wet not,—for Poseidon willed it so,
Honoring his son,—and all along their way
Was spread a perfect calm.   And every being
Of beauty or of mirth left his abode
Under the populous flood and journeyed with them.
Out of their deep green caves the Nereids came

Again to do him honor; shining limbs
And shining bosoms cleaving waked the main
All into sapphire ripples eachwhere crowned
With yellow tresses streaming.   Triton came
And all his goodly company, with shells
Pink-whorled and purple, many-formed, and made
Tumultuous music.   Ocean's tawny floor
They all left vacant, empty every bower,
And solitary the remotest courts.
Following in the midst of the array
Their mistress, her white horses paced along
Over the unaccustomed element,
Submissive, with the wonted chariot
Pillowed in vapors silver, pink, and gold,
Itself of pearl and fire.   And so they reached
Delos, and went together hand in hand
Up from the water and their company,
And the green wood received them out of sight.

ARIADNE.

I.

HUNG like a rich pomegranate o'er the sea
  The ripened moon; along the trancéd sand
The feather-shadowed ferns drooped dreamfully;
The solitude's evading harmony
  Mingled remotely over sea and land;
A light wind woke and whispered warily,
  And myriad ripples tinkled on the strand.

II.

She lay face downward on the sighing shore,
  Her head upon her bended arm; her hair
Loose-spreading fell, a heart-entangling store;
Her shoulder swelling through it glimmered more
  Divinely white than snows in morning air;
One tress, more wide astray, the ripples bore
  Where her hand clenched the ooze in mute despair.

30

III.

A wandering wind laughed over her, then slunk
  Shamefast away, laden with her deep woe,
Smit with the consciousness that she had drunk
Grief's numbing chalice to the dregs, and sunk,
  As deep as ever mortal soul could go,
To sleep's dim caves: while, like a wave-borne trunk,
  Did her still body no life-promise show.

IV.

Then stronger stirred her pulses; and a sound
  Of her deep-drawn and slowly-measured breath,
Now shattered by a gasping sob, or drowned
By sudden rustlings of the leaves around,
  Told of her spirit driven back from Death,
Whom it had sought with forehead duly bound
  With fillets, where the hemlock wavereth.

V.

A many-throated din came echoing
  Over the startled trees confusedly,
From th' inmost mountain folds hurled clamoring
Along the level shore to droop its wing:

She blindly rose, and o'er the moon-track'd sea
Toward Athens stretched her hands,—"With shouts
    they bring
Their conquering chieftain home; ah me! ah me!"

VI.

But clearer came the music, zephyr-borne,
  And turned her yearnings from the over-seas,
Hurtled unmasked o'er glade and belted bourne,—
Of dinning cymbal, covert-rousing horn,
  Soft waxen pipe, shrill-shouted EVOES:
Then sat she down unheeding and forlorn,
  Half dreaming of old Cretan melodies.

VII.

Like thought quick-frozen in the vivid brain
  At need of sudden, vast emergency,
She sat there dazed and motionless; the main
Sobbed round and caught her longest tress again,
  And clasped her shell-like foot, nor heeded she;
And nearer, and nearer, like thick gusts of rain,
  The clamor swelled and burst upon the sea:

VIII.

The thickets rocked; the ferns were trampled down;
  The shells and pebbles splashed into the waves;

The white sands reeked with purple stains and brown,
With crushed grape-clusters and fig-bunches strown ;
   Hoof'd sylvans, fauns, satyrs from mossy caves,
Fur-clad Bacchantes, leapt around to drown
   God Bacchus' voice, whose lip the crimson laves.

IX.

His thyrsus, wreathed with many-veinéd vine
   That magically blossomed and bare fruit,
He waved above the crowd with grace divine,
And straightway by the silver waste of brine
   They laid them gently down with gesture mute ;
The while he twinéd his persuasions fine
   And meshed her grief-clipt spirit with his lute.

X.

These sweet entanglements he closely wove,—
   " A god hath heard thy plainings piteous ;
A god's deep heart thy shrill shriek shuddering clove ;
A god hath left his incense-teeming grove,
   And sought thee by the chill sea's barrenness ;
A god's strong spirit night-long vainly strove,
   And fell before thy mortal loveliness.

XI.

" Forget the subtle-tongued Ionian's love,
   His speech that flowed like honey, and his vows ;

Forget the deaf, black ship that fleetly drove,
Leaving thee hopeless in this moaning cove;
  Forget the Past's dumb misery, and rouse
Thy heart and lift thy spirit clear above
  Dead griefs as fitteth godhead's promised spouse.

XII.

" And hearken, maiden !   I will love thee well.
  Then rise and follow, rise and follow, rise
And give a god thine hand, and come and dwell
With gods, and drink the purpling œnomel,
  And slake desire with aught that lures thine eyes,
From flowerful hermitage in some green dell
  To sphere-realms in the star-entangled skies.

XIII.

" Rich largess of all crystalline delights,
  With converse of the well-persuading lyre,
Shall satisfy thee of sweet sounds and sights,
And each compelling beauty that excites
  A yearning shall fulfil its own desire;
And vintagers shall worship thee with rites
  Of wine outpoured and vervain-nourished fire.

XIV.

" And all these pleasures shall be sure for thee;
  And woven through them like a golden thread

The certainty of one fixt love for thee,
And that a god's, shall bind them fast for thee,—
    So fast that by no finely-stinging dread,
Lest they should prove some dream-wrought mockery,
    Shall thy heart's joyance e'er be visited."

XV.

And so with silver-linkéd melodies
    He wooed her till the moon lay pale and low ;
And first she lifted up her dreaming eyes
And dreamed him her old love in fairer guise ;
    And then her soul drew outwards, and a glow
Woke in her blood of pleasure and surprise,
    To think it was a god that loved her so.

XVI.

And last she rose up happily, and gave
    Her hand to him, by sudden love made bold,—
The while the sun got up refreshed and drave
Square-shouldered through the lucent mists, that clave
    To the clear-echoed inland hills, and rolled
Along their peaks in many a pallid wave,
    Or floated coldly o'er the molten gold,—

XVII.

And went with him where honey-dew distils
    Through swimming air in odorous mists and showers,

Where music the attentive stillness fills, '
And every scent and color drips and spills
   From myriad quivering wings of orchid flowers;
And there they dwelt deep in the folded hills,
   Blissfully hunting down the fleet-shod hours.

XVIII.

And who shall say her love was incomplete?
   For love fares hardly on ingratitude,
And love dies quickly nurtured on deceit,
And love turns hatred captured by a cheat;
   And love had died while in despair immewed;
And this god's love was surely very sweet,
   For she was a forsaken maid he wooed.

LAUNCELOT AND THE FOUR QUEENS.

PART I.

Launcelot sleepeth under an apple-tree.

.

WHERE a little-trodden byway
Intersects the beaten highway
    Running downward to the river,
Stands an ancient apple-tree
In whose blossoms drowsily
    The bees are droning ever.

Back along the river's edge
Twists a tangled hawthorn hedge,
    In whose thickets lurks the thrush ;
Broods the skylark in the meads,
Floats the teal among the reeds,
    The warm wild-roses flush ;

The sundews clasp their glistening beads,
The sun in mid-sky reins his steeds,
  And languid noon enwraps the earth;
Scarce a living creature stirs,
Save some gadding grasshoppers
  That heedless prate their mirth.

'Neath the fruit-tree's latticed shade
An errant knight at length is laid,
  In opiate noon's deep slumber sunk;
His helm, well proved in conflicts stern,
Lies in a tuft of tender fern
  Against the mossy trunk.

A robin on a branch above,
Nodding by his dreaming love
  Whose four blue eggs are hatched not yet,
Winks, and watches unconcerned
A spider o'er the helm upturned
  Weaving his careful net.

The sleeper's hair falls curling fair
From off his forehead broad and bare,
  Entangling violets faint and pale;
Beside his cheek a primrose gleams,
And breathes her sweetness through his dreams,
  Till grown too sweet they fail.

PART II.

> And as he sleeps four queens come by
> And spy him 'neath the apple-tree.
> Of his fair show enamored sore
> They 'prison him by sorcery.

Hark, the voices blithe and gay !
Four queens of great estate are they,
And riding come they up this way,—
    Come they up from out the river ;
On four white horses do they ride,
And four fair knights do ride beside,
    As is their custom ever.

On upright spear each knight doth bear
One corner of an awning rare
Of silk, all green, and bordered fair
    With mystic-symbolled broidery ;
And o'er the ladies' milky-white,
Soft shoulders falls the tinted light,
    And nestles tremblingly.

Now come they where they well may see
The blossom-veiléd apple-tree.
Quoth Eastland's queen,—"It grieveth me
    That on the branch but blossoms are !

If it were only autumn now,
And apples crowned the stooping bough,
    I'd deem it fairer far:

" Drooping so ripe and melting mellow,
Rind-streaked red and flecked with yellow,
Each one fairer than its fellow,
    Oh, methinks I see them now!"
Thus quoth she; but Morgane le Fay
Hath cast her eyne another way,
    And peereth 'neath the bough.

" Now swear I on my life," quoth she,
" Fairer fruit is 'neath the tree
Than e'er will be upon the tree.
    See ye yon knight in armor black?
Can looks so brave and limbs so strong
To any lowlier knight belong
    Than Launcelot du Lac?

" Faith! we the fairest knight have found
That ever lady's arms enwound,
Or ever lady's kisses crowned;
    Myself can wish no royaller lover." . . .
" Nay! Think you then to choose for him,"
Quoth Eastland's queen, " while shadows dim
    His sheeny eyelids cover?

" Certes, 'twere discourtesie !
But put a spell of secrecy
Upon his drowsy eyne, till we
  May bring him to our magic towers ;
Then let him choose which one of us
Shall deck for him the amorous,
  Deep, blossom-scented bowers."

They weave a spell of witchery
Above his drowsy eyne, till he
Is breathing slow and heavily ;
  Then bear him homeward on his shield.
His war-horse neighs behind the hedge,
The duck drops back into the sedge,
  The lark into the field.

PART III.

He waketh in a chamber high,
 With tapestries adornéd fair ;
Unto a window climbeth up,
 And chanteth unto Guinevere.

In place of green o'ershadowing
  Launcelot sees above his head—
And, smiling, turns his magic ring—
A dragon fixt with brooding wing,
  And dismal claws outspread.

He gives the ring a prayerful turn,
      Which aye was wont to put to flight
All lying visions; but the stern,
Black dragon's eyeballs seem to burn
      With smouldering, inward light.

Now doth he slowly come aware
      No glamour 'tis, nor painted dream,
But oak, all carved with cunning care,
And for its eyes a sullen pair
      Of mighty jewels gleam.

From samite soft he lifts his head,
      Instead of earthy-scented moss;
Four walls he sees all fair bespread
With yellow satins, garnishéd
      With legends wrought across.

Half-hidden by a storied fold
      An archéd door he sees, shut close;
The sun, far-sunken o'er the wold,
Through archéd windows sluicing gold
      In sloping, moted rows,

Gleameth upon the topmost tier
      Of armor on the farther walls;
Shimmers in gules and argent clear;

Bathes the carven rafters bare;
Then seeks adown the ocean sheer
    His sleepless azure halls.

Now paleth silver on the floor
    In place of gold upon the roof;
From a young moon the still gleams pour,
That from the sun, her paramour,
    Yet walketh not aloof.

Where bars the window-niche emboss,
    Launcelot, climbing, chanteth clear;
His song it floateth soft across
The dreaming trees that fringe the foss,
    And seeketh Guinevere:

    " Hearken, Guinevere!
      Hear me, oh, my love!
    Waketh thy soul wistfully?
      Hither let it rove;
    Hither tripping swift
      O'er the silvered meadows,
    With whispers for my prisoned ears
      Fill the vacant shadows,
          Guinevere.

    " Hearken, Guinevere!
      Warm about my neck

Might I feel thy claspéd arms,
    Little would I reck
Prisonment or chains;
    Bitterer bonds hast thou
Link'd of rippled locks upon me,
    And I kiss them now,
                        Guinevere.

" Hearken, Guinevere !
    Spake thine eyes in silence,
As a stream that fareth softly
    Thorough summer islands ;
Uttered suddenly
    What I never guess'd,—
How I could betray my king
    At his queen's behest,
                        Guinevere.

" Hearken, Guinevere !
    Magic potenter
Than hath brought me to this plight
    Hath thy bosom's stir ;
Subtler witchery
    Hath thy whispering,
To make me foul before my God
    And false unto my king,
                        Guinevere.''

PART IV.

The queens essay to have his love;
  Denies he them disdainfully.
A damsel comes and pledges her
  For service due to set him free.

A dewy breeze laughs through the bars,
  With meadow scents and early light;
And soon appear the ladies fair
  In silken vestures richly dight:
" The noblest knight of Arthur's court
  We know thee for, Sir Launcelot !
Who, save for Lady Guinevere,
  For lady carest not.

" And now thou art our prisoner,
  And shalt lose her, and she lose thee ;
So it behoveth thee to choose
  One of us four for thy ladye.
And choose thou not, here shalt thou die.
  So choose : I am Morgane le Fay,
Here Eastland's queen, there she of the Isles,
  North Wales accepts *her* sway."

Saith he : " This is a grievous case,
   That either I must quit sweet life
Or keep it bitter with one of ye ;
   Yet liefer will I death to wife
With worship, than a sorceress,
   As ye are each, I'll lay me by.
What boots it that one's body live
   An' his dear honor die !"

" Is this your answer?" question they.
   "Yea, is it," laughs he carelessly.
Then go they sorely sorrowing,
   Leaving his spirit only free.
And training that to lonely flight,
   He seats him on his couch's side,
Till scent and song are heavy-winged
   About the hot noontide.

A breeze slips in refreshingly,
   As slowly swings the oaken door,—
Swings slow and lets a damsel in
   Bearing a most enticing store
Of fare to cheer his sinking heart,
   And set his slackened strings in tune,—
Collops of meat that taste of the woods,
   And mead that smells of June.

" Ill fareth it with thee, Sir Knight !"
  " Ne'er spakest thou a truer word,
Fair damsel," saith he, heavily,
  While up the walls the arras stirred.
Saith she : "This magic-bred mischance
  Shall vaunt not to have mastered thee ;
I'll see thee clearly quits with it
  And thou'lt be ruled by me."

" What service wouldst thou?" asketh he.
  " To help my father Tuesday next,
Who hath agreed a tournament
  Him and North Wales's king betwixt ;
For Tuesday last we lost the field."
  " Fair maid, who may thy father be ?
Needs is it that thou tell me this,
  Then will I answer thee."

" King Bagdemagus is his name."
  Saith he : " A knightly knight, and true,
And gentle ; by my body's faith
  I will thee willing service do."
She turns, and lifts the trencher up,
  And seeks the door with paces steady :
" When dripping Phosphor flickers gray
  Be ready."

PART V.

When western folds are flocked with stars,
  And larks are quivering up the blue,
Four clampéd doors, eleven locks,
  And seven gates, she leads him through.

The blue has killed the gray;
White fleeces swiftly stray
From the shepherd feet of day
    Over their azure pasture;
To their morning baths addrest,
The gusts with wrinkling zest
Over the river's breast
    Are following fast and faster.

The door swings open wide,
And quickly side by side
Adown the steps they glide
    To an iron-bolted gateway;
What Magic makes Truth mars;
And through her fortunate stars
These hell-forged bolts and bars
    Open before her straightway.

She brings him to his steed,
Hidden with mindful heed
Where mossy foot-paths lead
    From a broken pier on the river;

He draws his saddle-girth,
And tries his lance's worth,
Then canters with lightsome mirth
      Out from the thickets that quiver.

*   *   *   *   *   *

In primal sympathy
All nature laughed with glee,
Shouted to feel him free,
      Drank of his breath and kissed him ;
Nothing of sound and scent,
Color and coolness blent,
Nothing the morning meant
      In its myriad speeches missed him.

Over a knoll or two,
Grassy, and drenched with dew,
His blossomed pathway drew
      Till a screen between had risen ;
Then in his iron shoes
He rose and waved his "adieus :
"Methinketh neither I'll choose,
      Nor die in your witches' prison."

4

BALLAD OF THE POET'S THOUGHT.

A POET was vexed with the fume of the street,
  With tumult wearied, with din distraught;
And very few of the passing feet
  Would stay to listen the truths he taught:
  And he said,—"My labor is all for naught;
I will go, and at Nature's lips drink deep."—
  For he knew not the wealth of the poet's thought,
Though sweet to win, was bitter to keep.

So he left the hurry, and dust, and heat
  For the free, green forest where man was not;
And found in the wilderness' deep retreat
  That favor with Nature which he sought.
  She spake with him, nor denied him aught,
In waking vision or visioned sleep,
  But little he guessed the wealth she brought,
Though sweet to win, was bitter to keep.

50

But now when his bosom, grown replete,
   Would lighten itself in song of what
It had gathered in silence, he could meet
   No answering thrill from his passion caught.
   Then grieving he fled from that quiet spot,
To where men work, and are weary, and weep;
   For he said,—"The wealth for which I wrought
Is sweet to win, but bitter to keep."

ENVOI.

Oh, poets bewailing your hapless lot,
   That ye may not in Nature your whole hearts steep,
Know that the wealth of the poet's thought
   Is sweet to win, but bitter to keep.

A BALLAD OF THREE MISTRESSES.

FILL high to its quivering brim
    The crimson chalice, and see
The warmth and whiteness of limb
    Light-draped luxuriously ;
    Hark the voice love-shaken for thee,
My heart,—and thou liest ere long
    In the close captivity
Of wine, and woman, and song.

Though sweetly the dark wine swim,
    More sweet, more tyrannous she
Who, till the moon wax dim,
    Rules man from east sea to west sea.
    And strong tho' the red wine be,
Ne'ertheless is woman more strong,
    Most fair of the Jove-given three,—
Of wine, and woman, and song.

52

But the rhyme of thy Rhine-sung hymn
   Is more sweet than thyself, Lorelie !
As over the night's blue rim
   Thou chantest voluptuously ;
   So stronger is song for me
To bind with a subtiler thong,—
   Her only may I not flee
Of wine, and woman, and song.

ENVOI.

Then her must I serve without plea
   Who doeth her servants much wrong,
Queen Song of the Jove-given three,—
   Of wine, and woman, and song.

BALLAD TO A KINGFISHER.

KINGFISHER, whence cometh it
    That you perch here, collected and fine,
On a dead willow alit
    Instead of a sea-watching pine?
    Are you content to resign
The windy, tall cliffs, and the fret
    Of the rocks in the free-smelling brine?
Or, Kingfisher, do you forget?

Here do you chatter and flit
    Where bowering branches entwine,
Of Ceyx not mindful a whit,
    And that terrible anguish of thine?
    Can it be that you never repine?
Aren't you Alcyone yet?
    Eager only on minnows to dine,
O Kingfisher, how you forget!

To yon hole in the bank is it fit
   That your bone-woven nest you consign,
And the ship-wrecking tempests permit
   For lack of your presence benign?
   With your name for a pledge and a sign
Of seas calmed and storms assuaged set
   By John Milton, the vast, the divine,
O Kingfisher, still you forget.

ENVOI.

But here's a reminder of mine,
   And perhaps the last you will get;
So, what's due your illustrious line
   Now, Kingfisher, *do* not forget.

BALLAD OF A BRIDE.

BRING orange-blossoms fairly twined,
   Fair-plaited wreaths to wreathe her hair,
Sweet-smelling garlands meet to bind
   Her brows, and be out-glistened there ;
   Bring radiant blooms and jewels rare
Against the happy bridal day ;—
   A sound of parting thrills the air :—
Hearken a little to my lay.

Now, blossoms, shine! but ye shall find
   Beside her brow ye are not fair ;
Breathe sweetly an' ye have a mind,
   But with her breath can ye compare?
   Bright garlands, ye less lovely are,
Nathless adorn her while ye may,—
   Even now her thoughts are otherwhere :—
Hearken a little to my lay.

Now hasten, maids ; the flowers wind
   Amidst her hair with loving care ;
Wind roses, for their red consigned
   Beside her blushes to despair,
   Such happy beauty doth she wear ;
But haste,—her glad feet scarce will stay,
   Nor us she heeds, for *he* is near:—
Hearken a little to my lay.

ENVOI.

He comes, they go, a blissful pair ;
   Full willingly she speeds away ;
Full lightly heeds she this my prayer,—
   Hearken a little to my lay.

LOVE-DAYS.

The sweet-mouthed shore hath wed the singing sea,
    And winds are joyous with their kissing chime.
    The voice-beseeching rapture of the time
An utterance hath found in every tree,
        In bursts of happy rhyme.

All nature loves, and loves are all fulfilled.
    Me only hope deferred and waitings long
    Keep silent ; me these rich completions wrong :
Ah ! when shall I have leave my lips to gild
        With a sweet marriage-song ?

From scenes of glad love crownéd, long gone down
    The droning-billowed reaches of the years,
    The lotus-flutes are shrilling in mine ears,
And torches flash into mine eyes, and drown
        Their sight in envious tears.

58

All lovers surely now are satisfied,
　Save only we, whom yet no threshold waits,
　For whom not yet the inner temple's gates
Have lifted : how much longer must we bide,
　　　Pressing reluctant fates ?

Oh, too long tarryings make a weary way !
　Then kiss me, Love, and kiss me ; for the wings
　Of time are ever dropping divers things ;
And who may from the promise of to-day
　　　Guess what the morrow brings !

MEMNON.

I.

WEARY, forsaken by fair, fickle sleep,
   A traveller rose, and stood outside his tent,
That shrouded was in dusky shadows deep,
   By palm-trees cast that o'er it kindly leant.
   A low moon lingered o'er a large extent
Of lifeless, shifting sands; her pallid rays
   Had kissed the scorchéd waste to sweet content;
And now her farewells whispering, still she stays,
As loth to leave the land to Phœbus' fiery blaze.

II.

Slowly she sinks; and faint streaks quietly creep
   Up from the east into the dusky sky;
Aurora's yellow hair, that up the steep
   Streams to the rear of night full breezily,
Shaken from her flushed fingers that now dye
   60

The under-heavens crimson ; now she springs
    Full-blown before the Day, and hastens by
With silver-footed speed and yearning wings,
To kiss a form of stone that at her coming sings.

III.

Thrilled at the voice the traveller starts aside,
    And sees the image, prostrate, half enwound
With red, unstable sand-wreaths, and its wide
      Forehead, and lips that moved not with their sound
      Celestial, lined with many a furrowed wound,
Deep-graven by the gnawing desert blast :
      Half-buried sphinxes strewed the waste around,
And human-headed bulls, now mouldering fast,—
Their impious shapes half gone, their greatness wholly
      past.

IV.

Out of this desolation vast and dead,
    Now glorified and clothed in red and gold,—
Brightness befitting Egypt's hero's bed,—
      A matin to his goddess mother rolled
      From dawn-kissed lips, that also kissed the mould
Of their decaying substance. The sweet psalm
      Thrilled in the listener's ears, with manifold
Cool music mingled of the murmuring palm ;
And accents large and sad deepened the lifeless calm.

V.

"Sweet mother, stay; thy son requireth thee !
   All day the sun, with massive, maddening glare,
Beats on my weary brow and tortures me.
   All day the pitiless sand-blasts gnaw and wear
   Deep furrows in my lidless eyes and bare.
All day the palms stand up and mock at me,
   And drop cool shade over the dead bones there,
And voiceless stones, that crave no canopy :
O beautiful mother, stay; 'tis thy son prayeth thee.

VI.

"O mother, stay; thy son's heart needeth thee !
   The night is kind, and fans me with her sighs,
But knoweth not nor feeleth sad for me.
   Hyenas come and laugh into my eyes,
   The weak bats fret me with their small, shrill cries,
And toads and lizards crawl in slimy glee.
   Thou comest—and my tortures dost surprise—
And fondlest me with fresh hands tearfully.
O dewy-lipped mother, stay; thy son desireth thee.

VII.

"O mother, why so quickly wouldst thou flee ?
   Let Echo leave her mountain rocks and twine
My words with triple strength to cling to thee

And clog thy limbs from flight as with strong wine ;
    Let them recall sweet memories of thine,
Of how the long-shadowed towers of wind-swept Troy
    Were dear to thee, and near, whilst thou didst pine
For the god-faced Tithonus, and the joy
Thou drank'st when thou hadst gained the willing,
        kingly boy.

VIII.

" O mother, how Scamander chided thee,
    And swelled his tawny floods with grief for him,
And drowned his oozy rushes by the sea ;
    For often have I heard such tales from him,
    Thou listening, whilst the purple night did swim
Reluctant past, and young Æmathion hung
    Upon thy wealthy bosom ; music, dim
In ears not all divine, the nigh stars sung,
Of thine high origin Hyperion's courts among.

IX.

" O mother, what forebodings visited thee
    From the Laconian's ravish'd bridal bed ;
What mists of future tears half blinded thee
    When Ilion's god-built gates, wide-openéd,
    Let in the fatal Spartan woman wed
To Troy in flames, dogs gorged with Trojan slain,
    And tears of thine, mother, for thy son dead.

Dead ; would my soul were with the body slain,
Nor stony-fetter'd here upon this Theban plain !

X.

"O mother, what glooms darkened down on thee,
   And tearful fears made thy scared eyelids red,
When me thou sawest by some god's enmity
   Madly to meet Pelides' fury led,
   Sparing the agéd Nestor's childless head
By me made childless. On the Phrygian plain,
   Between the bright-eyed Greeks and Trojans bred
Warriors, I met the Phthian ash in vain,
Which bade my breast's bright wine the trampled
    stubble stain.

XI.

" Then, mother, weeping, thou to Jove didst flee,
   And wring thy fingers, and, a suppliant,
Didst kneel before him, grasping his great knee
   And awful beard, and clinging like a plant
   Of ivy to an oak, till he should grant
Peculiar honors, not vouchsafed before,
   To thy son's obsequies ; nor didst thou pant
And pray in vain, and kiss his beard all hoar,
And large ambrosial locks that veiled the sapphire
    floor.

XII.

"For, mother, when the ruddy-bosomed sea
   Had drunk its fill of fire, and, climbing high,
Smoke of my funeral-pyre, with savory
   Odors of oil and honey, 'riched the sky,
   Out of the seething flames a cloud did fly
Of shrill-voiced birds,—like swarms of swarthy bees
   That move their household gods in young July,—
And, screaming, fought and perished, to appease
My manes and fulfil impelling Jove's decrees.

XIII.

"O mother, hath my song no charm for thee,
   To hamper thee from flight? Thou then didst wait
Scarce till the lustral drops were dry for me,
   And embers parch'd with dark wine satiate ;
   But wast away through the Hesperean gate
To mourn o'er waters Atlantean.   Now
   Thy loose locks trailèd are in golden state
Down the far side of yon keen peaks of snow ;
The brazen sun hath come, and beareth on my brow.

XIV.

"Soon will for me the many-spangled night
   Rise, and reel round, and tremble toward the verge ;
Soon will the sacred Ibis her weird flight
   Wing from the fens where shore and river merge,

With long-drawn sobbings of the reed-choked surge.
The scant-voiced ghosts, in wavering revelry
   For Thebes' dead glory, gibber a fitful dirge:
Would thou wert here, mother, to bid them flee!
O beautiful mother, hear; thy chained son calleth
     thee."

RONDEAU.—"HESPER APPEARS."

HESPER appears when flowing gales
Have filled the sunset's fervid sails,
  When down the low dim orient hills
  The purple gloaming soft distils
To nestle in the crooning vales.

To fretted hearts whom want assails,
Whom Youth, nor Hope, nor Love avails
  To loose their wearying load of ills,
    Hesper appears,

Lifting the sordid dusty veils
That wrap us till our courage fails:
  Ah, vexéd hearts!   The hour fulfils
  Your yearnings with its peace, and stills
Awhile man's myriad fretful wails,—
    Hesper appears.

RONDEAU.—"WITHOUT ONE KISS."

WITHOUT one kiss she's gone away,
And stol'n the brightness out of day;
  With scornful lips and haughty brow
  She's left me melancholy now,
In spite of all that I could say.

And so, to guess as best I may
What angered her, awhile I stay
  Beneath this blown acacia bough,
    Without one kiss;

Yet all my wildered brain can pay
My questioning, is but to pray
  Persuasion may my speech endow,
  And Love may never more allow
My injured sweet to sail away
    Without one kiss.

RONDEAU TO A. W. STRATON.

(Written in his autograph album.)

To fledge the hours with mirth and ease
And wing their feet with pleasantries,
  Till heedlessly they hasten by
  As cloudlets down the summer sky,
Or bats mid twilight shadowed trees,

Or petals on the noontide breeze,
Full oft our laboring minds should please.
  So now to you I come to try
    To fledge the hours.

  And oft when they shall seem to lie
  Wingless and footless, we may buy
Wings for them from such names as these,
And happy-colored feathers seize
From their upspringing memories
    To fledge the hours.

THE FLIGHT.

SHE rose in the night and fled ;
   Such a night there was never another.
And her small hands shewed they red?
   What need ! It is cleanly to smother.
In warm arms sleeps the young wife,
And he fondles her,—" Love ! my life !"—
Ha ! ha ! but the child lies dead—
   Sweet dreams to you, father and mother !

Her hair streams out on the wind,
   The tree-tops wail and mutter,
The dry leaves patter behind,
   And before the gray bats flutter ;
Three crows are hastening after,—
But whence is that flying laughter?
She knows not, following blind,
   Nor heeds what the voices utter.

Down the long, moon-lighted glades
   Where the pale ghosts moan and shiver,
Through writhen, poisonous shades
   Where the night-shades heavily quiver ;
Where the reeking hollows are mute
She treads down the toad and the newt,
And thro' hemlock, sweet when love fades,
   She hastens, and rests not ever.

Shun yon thicket of grass !—
   A body lies there forgotten.
Strange it should come to pass
   Before the body is rotten.
They have crushed his head with a stone—
" Ha ! ha ! I am not alone."
And she flies ; while up the morass
   Roll the night-mists swamp-begotten.

Her light feet scale the crags
   Where the wild-goat scarce could follow,
And never her swift flight flags
   Till she reaches a yawn-mouthed hollow
Where a goodly company feast—
Of man, and devil, and beast,
And by torch-light revel the hags,
   And the beasts they grovel and wallow.

She comes among them by night,
   Her long hair over her falling,
Her white feet torn in her flight,
   And they gather around her brawling.
They shriek, they applaud, they groan,—
" Lady, we welcome our own.
Come and feast, thou hast won the right,—
   To wake him will need much calling."

ONE NIGHT.

THE wood is cold, and dank, and green ;
  The trunks stand close in sullen row ;
A crookéd moon through a creeping screen
  Of night-fog rots in the roots below.

The pool is thick, and dead, and green ;
  Its bubbles gleam the roots below ;
To feed the slimy growths between
  The slimy roots the ooze drips slow.

My feet can find no standing-place,
  The monstrous trunk my arms grasp not ;
Across the roots upon my face
  I fall, and pray my soul can not.

And one came by, and bare a load—
  An unstrange form—to where I lay ;
Into the pool he cast his load :
  "Look to it," he said, and went away.

73

The thick scum closed; the body slid
    Beneath the roots to where I lay,
And rose face up: I fain had hid
    My eyes; their lids forgot the way.

And fain my hands had hid my face,
    But could not quit their slimy hold;
Close to my face its loathly face
    Uprose, and back its swathings rolled.

Its dead eyes woke and with mine met
    Familiarly; at that I wept.
My tears fell big and fast, and set
    More foulness forth the scum had kept.

And more I wept more foul it grew;
    All else grew black, and my heart dropped down.
I had lain there for an age, I knew,
    And must lie there till the body sank down.

Then One came by to where I lay;
    He had heard my tears and come to me.
He had heard my tears (for I could not pray),
    And pitied me, and had come to me.

He touched the body, and it sank down
    Beyond my sight, though the pool was clear;

And the space above was a sapphire crown
   Upon their heads, for the trees to wear.

He stood me up upon my feet,
   And the trunks were dry and my hands were clean ;
The breath of laughing leaves was sweet :
   And he left me in this pleasant scene.

A SONG OF MORNING.

WEIRD Night has withdrawn
    Her gleaming black tresses,
        And, sighing for sorrow,
Has fled from the dawn,
Sinking her sleep-woven wings in the west,
    To breathe there her kisses
        On tired hearts that borrow
Her balm of sweet lethe and rest.

And Morning, upspringing
    From out the gray ocean
        With rosy-lipped laughter,
Her yellow locks flinging
O'er forest and fountain, field, fallow, and sky,
    With breezy, bright motion,
        Is hastening after,
While vapor-veiled glamours sail by.

76

ODE TO DROWSIHOOD.

BREATHER of honeyed breath upon my face!
  Teller of balmy tales! Weaver of dreams!
  Sweet conjurer of palpitating gleams
And peopled shadows trooping into place
        In purple streams
Between the drooped lid and the drowsy eye!
  Moth-winged seducer, dusky-soft and brown,
Of bubble gifts and bodiless minstrelsy
  Lavish enough! Of rest the restful crown!
At whose behest are closed the lips that sigh,
  And weary heads lie down.

Thee, Nodding Spirit! Magic Comforter!
  Thee, with faint mouth half speechless, I invoke,
  And straight uplooms through the dead centuries'
    smoke
The agéd Druid in his robe of fur,
        Beneath the oak
Where hang uncut the paly mistletoes.

The mistletoe dissolves to Indian willow,
Glassing its red stems in the stream that flows
  Through the broad interval ; a lazy billow
Flung from my oar lifts the long grass that grows
  To be the Naiad's pillow.

The startled meadow-hen floats off, to sink
  Into remoter shades and ferny glooms ;
    The great bees drone about the thick pea-blooms ;
The linkéd bubblings of the bobolink,
              With warm perfumes
From the broad-flowered wild parsnip, drown my brain ;
  The grakles bicker in the alder boughs ;
The grasshoppers pipe out their thin refrain
  That with intenser heat the noon endows :
Then thy weft weakens, and I wake again
  Out of my dreamful drowse.

Ah ! fetch thy poppy-baths, juices exprest
  In fervid sunshine, where the Javan palm
  Stirs scarce awakened from its odorous calm
By the enervate wind, that sinks to rest
              Amid the balm
And sultry silence, murmuring, half asleep,
  Cool fragments of the ocean's foamy roar,

And of the surge's mighty sobs that keep
  Forever yearning up the golden shore,
Mingled with song of Nereids that leap
  Where the curled crests downpour.

Who sips thy wine may float in Baiæ's skies,
  Or flushed Maggiore's ripples, mindless made
  Of storming troubles hard to be allayed.
Who eats thy berries, for his ears and eyes
          May vineyard shade
Melt with soft Tuscan, glow with arms and lips
  Cream-white and crimson, making mock at reason.
Thy balm on brows by care uneaten drips ;
  I have thy favors, but I fear thy treason.
Fain would I hold thee by the dusk wing-tips
  Against a grievous season.

ODE TO NIGHT.

I.

THE noon has dried thy dewdrops from my wings,
  My spirit's wings, so they no longer soar;
    And, drooping more and more,
I pant, O Night, for thy soft whisperings
  Of bounteous blessings which thou hast in store
    For me, and all who serve thee with due rites;
Not with a riotous loose merriment,
    That thy soft wrath excites;
But with sweet yielding to thy lavishment
Of warm syringa-scented breathings, blent
    With trancéd draughts of subtle-souled delights.

II.

Low-sighing zephyr, pulsing from the west,
  Before thee sheds earth-purifying dew,
    As priests were wont to do
With lustral waters, ere the victims, dressed
For sacrifice, felt the keen-searching knife.
      So

Then, thy light-fingered forager, and rife
  With thefts from all lush odors and sweet sounds,
    He drowses on thy skirt ;
Whilst thou, breast-full of new, sweet milk of life,
  Loosest the robe thy bounteous bosom bounds,
    With heart's-ease blooms and marigolds begirt.

III.

Dear goddess, come. Thy feather-sandalled feet
  Tread out the dying crimsons of the day,
    Whose warm, red-spirted spray
I'll find soft-changed to flushes rosy sweet,
Dowered by thee to my love's lips and cheeks :
My love, with whom is covert from the freaks
  Of Folly, so heart-vexing through the light,
    With whom a safe retreat,
In whose dusk bower sour Envy never speaks,
  Nor poison drips from venomed fangs of Spite ;
    Thither, dear Night, we'll haste on happy feet.

6

AMORIS VINCULA.

SUBTLER than all sorceries
This tender breath upon mine eyes;
Surer than steel, though soft as air,
These fetters of caressing hair;
Yet they gall not me, nor smart,
Heart-fast to a girlish heart.

Wakes upon the quiet night
Clamor of strife of might and right,
And bears unto a girlish ear
Vague messages of pain and fear,
And girlish arms more close enlace
To shield me in their weak embrace.

Ah, I too had girded me
And stood among the strong and free,—
Had struck, and shrunk not, for the right,
Amid the red death of the fight,—

Had fought and won, or fallen with them
That wear the hero's diadem.

I even now were smiting strong
In the front ranks, to smite the wrong,
But a girlish voice saith nay,—
Bids me stay, and I must stay :
Let Freedom rise, or faint, or fall,
Here is my faith, my fame, my all.

ITERUMNE?

Ah me!   No wind from golden Thessaly
  Blows in on me as in the olden days;
  No morning music from its dew-sweet ways,
No pipings, such as came so clear to me
Out of green meadows by the sparkling sea;
  No goddess any more, no Dryad strays,
  And glorifies with song the laurel maze;
Or else I hear not and I cannot see.

For out of weary hands is fallen the lyre,
  And sobs in falling; all the purple glow
    From weary eyes is faded, which before
Saw bright Apollo and the blissful choir
  In every mountain grove;—nor can I know
    If I shall surely see them any more.

AT POZZUOLI.

At Pozzuoli on the Italian coast
   A ruined temple stands.　The thin waves flow
   Upon its marble pavèments ; and in row
Three columns, last of a majestic host
Which once had heard the haughty Roman's boast,
   Rise in the mellow air.　Long years ago
   The unstable floor sank down.　Now from below
The shining flood of sapphire,—like the ghost

Of youth's bright aspirations and high hopes,
   More real than castles in the air, and laid
On some foundation, though of sand that slopes
   Seaward to lift again,—it comes arrayed
In olive sea-weeds ; but a raven mopes
   Upon its topmost stone, and casts a shade.

SAPPHO.

HER hair it floated fair and free
In the blushful evening sky;
    The purple sea
    Sobbed wearily,
To the curlew's mournful cry;
    Her white feet mock'd
    The barren rock,
With their warmth and beauty and life;
    Her white hands prest
    All close her breast,
To stifle its bursting strife.
    The musical sea
    Sobbed musically,
The warm wind whispered her,—"Flee:
    Counsel I thee
    That thou warily flee
The fair-seeming snare of the sea."

But deeper she drank,
As the gold sun sank,
The mist of the sea's purple breath ;
While the sun's last embrace
Lit flame in her face,
And her eyes searched the shadows of Death.

But the shadows are driven,
Like night-clouds riven,
From her eyes by a heaven of song,
That trembles and floats,
In silver-lipped notes,
From a light skiff drifting along :
All the singers save one
Full-faced to the sun,
But the one to the rim of the moon ;
And it seeméd the tune
Was the voice of the moon,
Or the moon the embodied tune.

O'er the tingling pink
Of her eager ear's brink
The golden melody swells,
As a ripple's song slips
In the dawn-kissed lips
Of listening, mimicking shells ;

And chases away—
So enchanting the lay—
Her purpose and pain, forsooth,
Till she sees the face,
In the thin moon's embrace,
Of the Mitylenian youth;
And the shadows return,
And her drooped lids burn,
And she calls to him under her breath;
Then leaps to meet,
At the cliff's chilled feet,
The hungry embraces of Death.

And the slumbrous sea
Wakes tremulously,
And thrills to his furthest streams;
And a sudden glow
Through the depths below
Gives the Nereids blissful dreams;
And the deepest sea-graves
In Leucadian caves
Are lighted with golden gleams,
As though the sunk sun
Had thitherward run
To pry with his fronting beams.

And the musical sea
Sings more musically
Than he ever has sung before,
And the whole night long
His syrenal song
Beguiles the soul of the shore.
And at peep of morrow
In red-eyed sorrow
The Lesbian maids come by ;
And search the sand
Of the rippled strand,
And the shallows remote and nigh ;
But they see the maiden
All tenderly laid in
A coral bed deep from harms ;
And for all their endeavor
The sea will not give her
From his encircling arms.
Nor ever could they
Have won her away,
For all their Ionian cunning,
Had not the sea-maids,
In their emerald braids,
Who were wont to sit a-sunning
In the sea-monarch's smile,
In their envy and guile

Upborn her again to the shore,
Which shall gleam with the blaze of her funeral-pile,
But throb with her song no more.

Chorus of Lesbian youth, singing around the funeral-pyre.

SEMI-CHORUS I.

Scatter roses from full hands;
  Wreathe bright garlands; bring white heifers.
Call sweet savors from far lands,
  Borne on wings of morning zephyrs.

SEMI-CHORUS II.

Burn, with olives' outpressed fatness,
  Riches of the swarthy bees.
Bring to slake the thirsty embers
  Wine new-purgéd from the leas.

SEMI-CHORUS I.

Twine the voices; wreathe the song;
  Weave a dirge of mythic numbers.

SEMI-CHORUS II.

Breathe it high and sweet and strong,
  For ye will not pierce her slumbers.

CHORUS.

Jove-bestowed, thy passioned singing
  O'er the Grecian nations came;
Was in Grecian ears a heaven,
  And in Grecian blood a flame.

Now thy songful lips are silent;
  But thy deathless song shall dwell
In men's bosoms, and its echoes
  Down far-distant ages swell.

And forever thy sweet singing
  Rich to hearts of men shall come,
In its meaning and its music
  A full goblet crowned with foam.

Now the sea lies gray and chilly
  Under the wet streaks of dawn;
Now the dull red embers darken,
  And their glow is almost gone:

Quench them; pour the last libation;
  Slake them with red Lesbian wine;
In wrought brass enclose her ashes:
  Once more are the Muses nine.

MIRIAM.—I.

SAPPHICS.

MIRIAM, loved one, were thy goings weary?
Journeyed not with thee one to brighten thy way?
Lighted with love-light how could it be dreary?
    Was it not my way?

Why wert thou weary? All the golden glories
Streaming from love's lamp thy enraptured sight won;
Sweetly we whispered old self-heroed stories,
    Miriam, bright one!

Crimson lipp'd love-flowers sprang about us going,
Clustering closely, rosy shadows weaving;
Straight from our footsteps glowing ways were flowing,
    Vistas far-cleaving.

92

Silvery lute-notes thrilled athrough the noonlight,
Flutings of bird-throats light as flight of swallow ;
Scents rose around us thick as in the moonlight
    Leaves fall and follow.

How could I dream that thou wert growing weary?
Never I guessed it till I saw thee fading ;
Saw thee slip from me,—and my way fell dreary.
    Cease thine upbraiding !

Cease thine upbraiding, ah, my widowed spirit !
Trace on thy path by rays from backward sight won.
More than I gave thee the bliss thou dost inherit,
    Miriam, bright one !

MIRIAM.—II.

CHORIAMBICS.

AH, Love, what would I give just for a little light!
  Cryings born of the wind wake on its undertones.
Vainly praying the shore wearily all the night
    Round me the ocean moans.

Ebb-tides laden with woe flee with a wailful song
  Far down out of the dark, calling my trembling soul.
Ah, Love, where is the light? Why is the way so
    long? . . .
    Hearken how sad their roll!

Ay, sad surely, but sweet! Why do they always call,—
  All night through the thick dark calling me out to
    thee?
Lured by surf-whispers soft, feebly my footsteps fall
    Toward the enfolding sea.
    94

Nay! I cover my ears; 'tis not the way to thee.
  Why doth it play me false now that my paths are
    blind?
When they lay in the light born of thy love to me,
  Never it seemed unkind.

Sweet it sang in the light, scarce could it dream a
    dirge;
  Fringed with ripples of blue tinkled the strand like
    bells;
When, thy hand in my hand, crushed we along its
    verge
    Pebbles and pink-lipp'd shells.

Ah! but full were the hours, full to the heart's desire;
  Flowing over with love, golden their flying feet.
Deep and sweet was the air, shining and clear like fire,
  Vital with balmy heat.

Warm,—but now it is cold; bright,—it is wild and
    dark;
  Dimly over the sea lieth the gleamless pall;
Dimly out of the sea murmur the voices. Hark!
    Do not they sweetly call?

Stay me, Miriam, Love; chill is the drifting foam.
  Come, Love, meet me with strength; fierce is the
    moaning sea.
Peace! peace! vainly I call; thou wilt not quit thy
    home;
  Wait; I will come to thee.

A BLUE BLOSSOM.

A SMALL blue flower with yellow eye
  Hath mightier spell to move my soul
  Than even the mightiest notes which roll
From man's most perfect minstrelsy.
  A flash, a momentary gleam,
  A glimpse of some celestial dream,
And tears alone are left to me.

Filled with a longing vague and dim,
  I hold the flower in every light ;
  To purge my soul's redarkened sight
I grope till all my senses swim.
  In vain ; I feel the ecstasy
  Only when suddenly I see
This pale star with the sapphire rim.

Nor hath the blossom such strange power
  Because it saith " Forget me not"
  For some heart-holden, distant spot,
Or silent tongue, or buried hour.

Methinks immortal memories
Of some past scenes of Paradise
Speak to my spirit through the flower.

Forgotten is our ancient tongue ;
    Too dull our ears, our eyes too blind,
    Even quite to catch its notes, or find
•Its symbols written bright among
    All shapes of beauty.   But 'tis hard,
    When one *can* hear, to be debarred
From knowledge of the meaning sung.

THE SHANNON AND THE CHESA-
PEAKE.

OH, shout for the good ship Shannon,
  And cheer for the gallant Brooke,
For hot was the fight she fought
  And staunch the ship he took.

When the might of the land was astonished,
  And wreck on wreck had gone down,
The old flag fast at the peak,
  But the old flag's fame o'erthrown,

Then Brooke in the good ship Shannon
  Set it forth in face of the world
That "hearts of oak" still flourished
  To keep the old flag unfurled.

'Twas the fair-starred first of June,
  A day of glorious days,
When York and Penn drove the Dutch,
  And Howe put the French to amaze;

And out from Boston Harbor
   The frigate Chesapeake steered ;
Not a sound save the wash on her bows,
   Till her crew broke silence and cheered.

In curt return from the Shannon
   Came a round shot over the rail,
And sullenly, one by one,
   Fell the first of the deadly hail.

Then full in its blind, white thunder
   Burst the wrath of that iron rain,
Sweeping the broad decks bare
   Till their timbers staggered again.

And the men crouch down for their lives,
   And the heavy pall of the smoke
Is rent by the fierce, red flashes
   And the splinter's hurtling stroke.

Hot work at the belching cannon,
   In the sweat, and powder, and grime,
Till the Chesapeake's steersman falls,
   And firing slacks for a time ;

For she drops afoul of our quarter,
   And her gallant captain dies.

Grapple now, for her mightiest bulwark
　　Is fallen where Lawrence lies.

We swarm in over the taffrail,
　　With hot strokes taken and given,
And Brooke at our head, till the foe
　　To the hold or the chains are driven.

We haul down the "Stars and Stripes;"
　　But, oh, the grief and the woe!—
A matter of twisted halliards,
　　And the storm-worn flag *below*.

But it costs us dear, that blunder,
　　For our gunner misunderstands,
And Watt and five brave seamen
　　Take death at their comrades' hands.

But, hark you, there is the summons!
　　And sullenly they comply.
Brave men; they fought till hope perished,
　　But better surrender than die.

Now cheer for the good ship Shannon,
　　And the good fight fought that morn,
For the old flag's vindication,
　　And its ancient honor upborne!

But woe must be in such warfare,
   Though lost be the battle or won,
For brother's slaughter of brother
   And father smitten of son.

Pray God that England no more
   Stand wroth from her daughter apart !
Pray God one blood and one tongue
   Be one in hand and in heart !

But let a great wrong cry to heaven ;
   Let a giant necessity come ;
And now, as of old, she can strike,
   She will strike, and strike home.

THE MAPLE.

Oh, tenderly deepen the woodland glooms,
  And merrily sway the beeches;
Breathe delicately the willow blooms,
  And the pines rehearse new speeches;
The elms toss high till they brush the sky,
  Pale catkins the yellow birch launches,
But the tree I love all the greenwood above
  Is the maple of sunny branches.

Let who will sing of the hawthorn in spring,
  Or the late-leaved linden in summer;
There's a word may be for the locust-tree,
  That delicate, strange new-comer;
But the maple it glows with the tint of the rose
  When pale are the spring-time regions,
And its towers of flame from afar proclaim
  The advance of Winter's legions.

And a greener shade there never was made
   Than its summer canopy sifted,
And many a day as beneath it I lay
   Has my memory backward drifted
To a pleasant lane I may walk not again,
   Leading over a fresh, green hill,
Where a maple stood just clear of the wood—
   And oh, to be near it still!

TO WINTER.

RULING with an iron hand
O'er the intermediate land
Twixt the plains of rich completeness,
And the realms of budding sweetness,
Winter ! from thy crystal throne,
With a keenness all thy own
Dartest thou, through gleaming air,
O'er the glorious barren glare
Of thy sunlit wildernesses,
Thine undazzled level glances,
Where thy minions' silver tresses
Stream among their icy lances ;
While thy universal breathing,
Frozen to a radiant swathing
For the trees, their bareness hides,
And upon their sunward sides
Shines and flushes rosily
To the chill pink morning sky.

Skilful artists thou employest,
And in chastest beauty joyest,—
Forms most delicate, pure, and clear,
Frost-caught starbeams fallen sheer
In the night, and woven here
In jewel-fretted tapestries.
But what magic melodies,
As in the bord'ring realms are throbbing,
Hast thou, Winter?—Liquid sobbing
Brooks, and brawling waterfalls,
Whose responsive-voicéd calls
Clothe with harmony the hills,
Gurgling meadow-threading rills,
Lakelets' lisping wavelets lapping
Round a flock of wild ducks napping,
And the rapturous-noted wooings,
And the molten-throated cooings,
Of the amorous multitudes
Flashing through the dusky woods,
When a veering wind hath blown
A glare of sudden daylight down?—
Naught of these!—And fewer notes
Hath the wind alone that floats
Over naked trees and snows;
Half its minstrelsy it owes
To its orchestra of leaves.
Ay! weak the meshes music weaves

For thy snaréd soul's delight,
'Less, when thou dost lie at night
'Neath the star-sown heavens bright,
To thy sin-unchokéd ears
Some dim harmonies may pierce
From the high-consulting spheres :
'Less the silent sunrise sing
Like a vibrant silver string
When its prison'd splendors first
O'er the crusted snow-fields burst.
But thy days the silence keep,
Save for grosbeaks' feeble cheep,
Or for snow-birds' busy twitter
When thy breath is very bitter.

So my spirit often acheth
For the melodies it lacketh
'Neath thy sway, or cannot hear
For its mortal-cloakéd ear.
And full thirstily it longeth
For the beauty that belongeth
To the Autumn's ripe fulfilling ;—
Heapéd orchard-baskets spilling
'Neath the laughter-shaken trees ;
Fields of buckwheat full of bees,

Girt with ancient groves of fir
Shod with berried juniper;
Beech-nuts mid their russet leaves;
Heavy-headed nodding sheaves;
Clumps of luscious blackberries;
Purple-cluster'd traceries
Of the cottage climbing-vines;
Scarlet-fruited eglantines;
Maple forests all aflame
When thy sharp-tongued legates came.

Ruler with an iron hand
O'er an intermediate land !
Glad am I thy realm is border'd
By the plains more richly order'd,—
Stock'd with sweeter-glowing forms,—
Where the prison'd brightness warms
In lush crimsons thro' the leaves,
And a gorgeous legend weaves.

EPISTLE TO W. BLISS CARMAN.

September, 1878.

An azure splendor floats upon the world.
Around my feet the blades of grass, impearled
And diamonded, are changing radiantly.
At every step new wonders do I see
Of fleeting sapphire, gold, and amethyst,—
Enchanting magic of the dew sun-kissed.
The felon jay mid golden-russet beeches
Ruffles his crest, and flies with startled screeches.
Ever before me the shy cricket whistles
From underneath the dry, brown, path-side thistles.
His gay note leads me, and I quickly follow
Where dips the path down through a little hollow
Of young fir-seedlings.   Then I cross the brook
On two gray logs, whose well-worn barkless look
Tells of the many black-gown-shadowed feet
Which tread them daily, save when high June's heat
Scatters us wide, to roll in cool salt billows
Of Fundy's make, or under hanging willows

109

Slide the light birch, and dream, and watch the grasses
Wave on the interval as the light wind passes,
Puffing a gentle cloud of smoke to scare
The sand-flies, which are ravening everywhere.
  Such our enjoyment, Bliss, few weeks ago ;
And the remembrance warms me with a glow
Of pleasure, as I cross the track and climb
The rocky lane I've clambered many a time.
On either side, where birch and maples grow,
The young firs stand with eager hands below,
And catch the yellow dropping leaves, and hold
Them fast, as if they thought them dropping gold ;
But fairy gold they'll find them on the morrow,
When their possessing joy shall turn to sorrow.
  Now thro' the mottled trunks, beneath the boughs,
I see the terrace, and the lower rows
Of windows drinking in the waking air ;
While future Freshmen stand around and stare.

*   *   *   *   *   *   *

Last week the bell cut short my happy strain.
Now half in pleasure, half in a vague pain,
For you I undertake my rhyme again.
Last week in its first youth saw you begin
Your happy three-years' course with us, and win
The highest honors, half of which are due
To your own strength of brain, and half accrue

To that wise master from whose hands you came
Equipped to win, and win yourself a name.
But I,—I have but one quick-slipping year
To spend amid these rooms and faces dear,
And then must quit this fostering roof, these walls,
Where from each door some bright-faced memory calls,
And halt outside in sore uncertainty,
Not knowing which way lies the path for me
Through the unlighted, difficult, misty world.
Ah, whither must I go?   Thick smoke is curled
Close round my feet, but lifts a little space
Further ahead, and shews to me the face—
Distorted, dim, and glamourous—of Life ;
With many ways, all cheerless ways, and rife
With bristling toils crowned with no fitting fruit,—
All songless ways, whose goals are bare and mute.
But *one* path leads out from my very feet,—
The only one which lures me, which is sweet.
Ah ! might I follow it, methinketh then
My childhood's brightest dreams would come again.
Indeed, I know they dwell there, and I'd find
Them meeting me, or hastening up behind.
See where it windeth, alway bright and clear,
Though over stony places here and there ;
Up steep ascents, thro' bitter obstacles,
But interspersed with glorious secret dells ;

And vocal with rich promise of delight,
And ever brightening with an inward light
That soothes and blesses all the ways that lie
In reach of its soft light and harmony.
And were this path made for my following,
Then would I work and sing, and work and sing;
And though the songs were cryings now and then
Of me thus singing in the midst of men,—
Where some are weary, some are weeping, some
Are hungering for joys that never come;
And some drive on before a bitter fate
That bends not to their prayers importunate;
Where some say God is deaf and hears not now,
And speaks not now, some that He *is* not now,
Nor ever was, and these in fancied power
See not the mighty workings of each hour,
Or, seeing, read them wrong. Though now and then
My songs were wailings from the midst of men,
Yet would I deem that it were ever best
To sing them out of weariness to rest;
Yet would I cheer them, sharing in their ills,
Weaving them dreams of waves, and skies, and hills;
Yet would I sing of Peace, and Hope, and Truth,
Till softly o'er my song should beam the youth,—
The morning of the world. Ah, yes, there hath
The goal been planted all along that path;

And as the swallow were my heart as free,
Might I but hope that path belonged to me.

I've prated so, I scarce know what I've said;
But you'll not think me to have lost the thread,
Seeing I had none.   Do not say I've kept
My promises too amply, and o'erleapt
A letter's bounds; nor harshly criticise;
But miss the spots and blots with lenient eyes.
Scan not its outer, but its inner part;
'Twas not the head composed it, but the heart.

8

DEDICATION.

THESE first-fruits, gathered by distant ways,
In brief, sweet moments of toilsome days,
   When the weary brain was a thought less weary,
And the heart found strength for delight and praise,—

I bring them and proffer them to thee,
All blown and beaten by winds of the sea,
   Ripened beside the tide-vext river,—
The broad, ship-laden Miramichi.

Even though on my lips no Theban bees
Alighted,—though harsh and ill-formed these,
   Of alien matters in distant regions
Wrought in the youth of the centuries,—

Yet of some worth in thine eyes be they,
For bare mine innermost heart they lay ;
   And the old, firm love that I bring thee with them
Distance shall quench not, nor time bewray.

   FREDERICTON, July, 1880.